DATE DUE

GAYLORD			PRINTED IN U.S.A.

2208
Gypsy in the Cellar

Bonnie Highsmith Taylor
AR B.L.: 3.3
Points: 3.0   MG

Gypsy in the Cellar

by Bonnie Highsmith Taylor

Cover Illustration: Dea Marks
Inside Illustration: Dea Marks

For my grandmother Sedenia Griffin

Perfection Learning® Corporation
1000 North Second Avenue, P.O. Box 500
Logan, Iowa 51546-0500.
Phone: 800-831-4190 • Fax: 712-644-2392
Paperback ISBN 0-7891-5112-x
CoverCraft® ISBN 0-7807-9054-5

4 5 6 7 8 9 10 PP 08 07 06 05 04

Contents

1

Gypsy Life

My name is Doreen, and I am a Gypsy. I live with my grandmother and my brother, Frankie. Also my Uncle Alex and the woman he married last summer. And she has three kids that live with us too.

I hardly remember my mother. She died when I was only five. I'm not sure where my father is. But I think he's in jail.

I asked Grandmother about my father. She said, "It makes no difference. You have a family."

When I ask Uncle Alex, he just laughs. "I'll be your father for ever and ever," he always says. Uncle Alex was in jail once. But only for a little while.

I don't live any certain place. Gypsies like to travel around. It's nice in the summers. We camp most of the time at the edge of small towns or in the woods by rivers and streams. Lots of families camp together. So there are plenty of kids to play with.

When it's warm, we sleep on the ground under the sky. I like to lie awake and look at the moon and stars.

Sometimes when everyone else is asleep, I sing to myself. I guess there's not much I like better than singing. Especially at night when there's a little breeze blowing. It sounds so good.

One night I was lying awake singing, and a cat came into our camp. It climbed right in bed with me! I held it tight for a long time. Then it scratched me, so I slapped it. And then it ran off.

Cats carry ringworms. Frankie and I had ringworms once. They're awful. Frankie had to have all his hair cut off. He looked like a little, old, bald man.

The school nurse made us stay out of school for the rest of the year. That part was nice. I don't like school very much. I've been to a lot of schools. They're all the same. Besides, most of them are in the city.

In the winters we usually have to live in the city. We live in empty store buildings most of the time. Sometimes we live in motor courts. But store buildings are better. They don't cost as much. And they are so big that three or four families can live together.

One time we lived in a house. For three days, I think. It was a beautiful house. It had beds that were off the floor. And it had a stove that cooked with the turn of a knob. Grandmother was scared of the stove.

"It's an evil spirit!" she screamed when Uncle Alex made the flame go high.

Uncle Alex and Frankie laughed at her. I tried to laugh. But I was really scared of it too.

It was in the middle of the night when the police came. They didn't knock or anything. They just broke in the door. Then they started pulling us out of bed and swearing at us.

I fell and bumped my head on a chair. My head started bleeding.

Grandmother flew at one of the policemen. She scratched his face and tore some buttons off his coat. He called her a bad name and pushed her down. Another one put handcuffs on Uncle Alex.

"Filthy Gypsies!" they yelled. "Dirty, sneaking thieves! We'll see to it the owners press charges when they get back."

That was when Uncle Alex went to jail. They were going to put Grandmother in jail. But one of the policemen said, "Then the welfare will be stuck with these two." He looked right at Frankie and me. "Lice and filth and all. They'll have to fumigate the house as it is."

7

I hated policemen after that. They were another thing that was bad about the city. The city was full of *Gajos*. Gajos are people who aren't Gypsies. I hated all of them. Well, I did until last fall.

The rains had started. We had to leave the nice place out in the country and move to a city I had never been to before. Uncle Alex and Grandmother had been there but not for a long time.

Grandmother didn't like the fall. It rained so much that it made her rheumatism worse. Even the little bag of burdock seeds she wore around her neck didn't help.

But Uncle Alex said it was a good place to make a living. His new wife had relatives there, and she liked it.

The store building we moved into was small. Smaller than most of the others we had lived in. Grandmother draped her old bedspread and curtains in one corner by the window. That made it very crowded. And hardly any light shone in at all.

The corner was for Grandmother's *ófisa*. This was where she told fortunes. Grandmother was a *dukkerer*.

Gypsy women can get a fortune-telling license at the city hall. Then the police don't give them any trouble. Just as long as they don't cheat the Gajos. But Gajos are easy to cheat. They think Gypsies are stupid.

Grandmother's fortune-telling name was Madame Sedenia. My mother had been a dukkerer. I guess I will be too, when I'm grown. It is the best way for a Gypsy woman to make a living. I have already practiced telling fortunes on Frankie and some of the other younger children.

One time I foretold that Frankie would go on a long journey and face great danger. And guess what—he did! He hitched a ride on a streetcar and got lost in the other end of town. A policeman and a truant officer brought him home late that night.

They threatened Grandmother. "See that the child is sent to school and kept off the streets," they ordered. "Or the welfare will take him away."

Grandmother wept and threw herself into the arms of the truant officer. "Oh, please, kind one," she begged. "The child will be justly punished and sent to school every day."

After the two men left, she held Frankie close and laughed. "Bad boy, you got caught." Then she shook her fist at the closed door and shouted, "Rotten Gajos!"

When she opened her fist, I saw something bright and shiny. There were initials on it. It was a cigarette lighter. Grandmother smiled and buried it deep in the pocket of her skirt.

Our new home was very small. Only our family lived there. But there were other Gypsy families, friends, and relatives close by, some in the same block.

For the first week, it rained nearly every day. Most of the time Frankie, our new cousins, and I sat by the stove and played games.

In between showers the boys would go outside. They'd pick up empty cigarette packages on the sidewalk. We saved the tin foil. We sold it to the junkman when he came around on Saturdays.

Selling tin foil and milk bottles is a good way for Gypsy kids to make money. Milk bottles are worth a nickel apiece.

Sometimes we would press the foil around small rocks or chips of brick. This made it weigh heavier. And the junkman would pay more than it was worth. But if he found out, he would not pay us at all. And he would keep the foil.

Sometimes a junkman would buy the tin foil without suspecting he was being cheated. Then we could not resist taunting him from a safe distance. "Rock buyer! Rock buyer! Stupid Gajo!"

Then we would run up an alley and hide under a stairway. Or behind a row of trash cans.

Sometimes the junkmen would call the police. But usually they were too ashamed to admit they had been tricked. And besides, all Gypsy kids look alike to Gajos.

If only it would stop raining. It was so cold, and I was tired of staying inside. I wanted to go out and look the new neighborhood over. I shivered and scooted closer to the stove. The boys were getting very loud in their game of jacks.

Aunt Wanda scolded them from the other corner. She and Cousin Rosa were busy making a new quilt. "If you can't play more quietly, you must find something else to do. Perhaps you would like to cut quilt blocks like girls."

The boys lowered their voices at once.

I knew I should be helping my aunt and Rosa. But I was so cold. I pulled my sweater tighter around my body and began to sing softly.

From inside the curtained room, Grandmother called, "Louder, Doreen. Sing louder. Such a voice, like the trill of the wild canary."

I smiled and sang louder. How I loved to sing! It made me forget everything. The rain, the cold, the musty darkness of the building. My voice echoed against the high walls.

"Like the tinkling of a hundred tiny bells," Grandmother murmured.

Even the boys stopped their game of jacks and listened.

Suddenly there was the sound of a real bell that hung over the front door. A tall, red-haired woman came in. Grandmother pulled back the curtain and greeted her. "Come in. Come in. Welcome to the ófisa of Madame Sedenia."

Grandmother had a customer.

Now if only Uncle Alex could find a job.

2

The Pickle Incident

The next day it stopped raining. But it was still cold in the morning unless we stayed in the sun. I put on my sweater and one of Rosa's jackets. The jacket was so big I had to roll up the sleeves. But it kept me warm.

Little Cousin Nicky was sick. Grandmother had been up half the night doctoring him. The place still smelled from the sulphur that she had burned on top of the stove. Nothing could make him stop throwing up. I thought the sulphur made it worse. It almost made *me* throw up.

Grandmother made us eat a big breakfast of cornmeal mush and sardines. She gave Frankie, my cousin George, and me a sip of her wine. "To warm your blood," she said.

I wished I had an orange. But they were all gone. Grandmother had packed the last one in Uncle Alex's lunch. He had a job for the day loading briquettes. He would probably bring home a few briquettes, as well as his wages.

"I'll get you an orange at the fruit stand," Frankie promised.

Frankie, George, and I started off together.

Rosa stayed home to help her mother. She was 13, almost a grown-up. And it was time for her to learn things like cooking and sewing. There were more quilts to be made before winter came.

"Let's go past the school first," suggested George. "Rosa and I went there once when we stayed with Mama's sister. Right after Papa died."

"No!" protested Frankie. "They'll see us and make us go. I don't want to go to school. I hate it!"

"Me too," I said. "Stupid Gajo teachers! Stupid Gajo kids!"

"We'll stay out of sight," said George. "All the teachers are old women. We can outrun them."

"But what about the truant officers?" Frankie asked fearfully. We'd had a lot of experience with truant officers. "They report you to the welfare."

"Aw, they don't really," George said. "They just say that to scare you."

I didn't want to go by the school any more than Frankie did. But I didn't want to admit that I was scared.

I was hoping we wouldn't have to go to school this year. Grandmother didn't care much. As long as we didn't get reported, we were safe.

Uncle Alex thought we should go to school regularly. But that was because he could read and write.

Once Uncle Alex read a whole book to Frankie and me. The name of it was *Mary Poppins*.

Uncle Alex had painted a bookstore. And the owner said Uncle Alex could have the book. He gave it to me for my birthday.

Mary Poppins was a really good book. I think Mary Poppins was a Gypsy. She did a lot of magic things.

I was going to read it myself someday. But Grandmother said it must have gotten lost in all of our moves. Besides, when I try to read, I have to skip so many words that I don't know. Then the story doesn't make much sense.

We didn't go on the school yard. We stood on the sidewalk for a while and just watched.

Then the whistle blew for morning recess. We ducked into some bushes. About a hundred kids came running out and scattered in all directions. Most of them ran for the swings and slides. Some started a ball game. A bunch of them just ran around. They were yelling and jumping like they were glad to get outside.

I could see a few Gypsy kids. But they stayed off by themselves. It looked like they were doing some trading.

After the kids went back in, we got tired of hanging around. So we started back toward the markets. Women were everywhere doing their shopping.

"Be ready to run," George warned. "One of them will be sure to ask why we aren't in school."

"Yeah," Frankie agreed. "Women are worse than men. They like to stick their nose in your business. Men don't care too much if you go to school or not. Unless they're truant officers. And that's because of the reward."

"Reward!" I gasped. "What reward?"

"For every kid they catch," Frankie said. "They get a hundred dollars for every kid they take back to school. Two hundred dollars for a Gypsy kid."

"Gee!" I said. "I didn't know that."

I don't think George knew it either. He looked real surprised.

"Hey, look," said Frankie. "Dill pickles. Sure wish I had one."

There was a big barrel of pickles in front of the butcher shop. Dills were two for a nickel. And you could usually pick out your own.

"I've got three cents," George said. He pulled three pennies out of his pocket.

"I've got two cents in my shoe," I said. "I was saving it for a ladyfinger at the bakery. But a dill pickle sounds awful good." I pulled off my shoe and handed the money to George.

"How about you?" he asked my brother.

Frankie shook his head. "Nothing."

"I'll see if I can get three small ones instead of two big ones," George said.

We walked up to the butcher. "We want some pickles," said George.

The butcher turned around. He looked at us like we were going to rob him. "You got money?" he snapped.

George showed him the five pennies. "Can we have three little ones instead of two big ones?"

"Don't have any little ones," the butcher said. "They're all big. Two for a nickel."

The butcher took a long fork and speared a pickle. Then he dropped it into a white paper carton. When he started to get the second one, George said, "That one, mister. That big fat one." He pointed into the barrel.

The man moved his fork.

"No, no," George said. "That one, right there."

The man moved his fork again. "Where?" he asked impatiently. "They're all the same."

"Let me get it," said George.

Before the man could protest, George grabbed the fork. He started jabbing it around in the barrel. "Here," he said, dropping another pickle into the carton. "It's a big one."

George gave him the pennies. The man closed the carton and handed it to him.

"Don't hang around here now," grumbled the man. "And don't come back again unless you have money."

Frankie, George, and I walked down the street. We stopped in front of a fruit stand. There was an empty orange crate on the sidewalk. We sat down, and George opened the carton. He handed me a pickle and bit into the other one.

"Where's mine?" Frankie asked.

George laughed. He stretched out his sweater sleeve and shook his arm. Frankie's pickle slid out.

It was warm in the sun. It felt good just to sit there, sucking our pickles. Even without looking, I could feel the people in front of the stand staring at us. At first we could tell they were whispering. But after a while they talked loud enough that we could hear them.

"Dirty! I've heard they always have lice," said one stout old woman.

"Every winter they come back. Don't seem to ever

settle down in one place," her friend replied, holding an umbrella.

"And they'd rather steal than work. Steal the socks right off your feet," said a third lady. She stood with her fat arms crossed and a look of disapproval on her face.

Frankie giggled. "Sure wouldn't want her old socks. Couldn't get them off her big feet anyway."

"Be quiet," I said, poking my brother.

I didn't think it was funny. I got all choked up inside with hating them. I could remember schoolteachers talking like that right in front of me. Like I wasn't even there. I hated them all.

I was glad George had stolen that old pickle. If the man had picked them both out, he would have cheated us. Given us the two smallest ones in the barrel. Or one that was soft.

Frankie crammed the last bite of pickle in his mouth. He pulled off his hat and scratched his head.

"Look!" one of the old women gasped in horror. "What did I tell you? That child's got lice as sure as I'm standing here."

"What's lice?" asked Frankie.

"Little bugs that crawl around in your hair," I explained. "Uncle Alex says you get them from animals and dirty places."

Frankie grinned and scratched his head again. Then

he pinched his thumb and finger together. He squinted his eyes like he was looking at something.

"Got him!" he yelled. "That's a big one!"

George giggled. He started scratching his head. "Look at this one!" he exclaimed. "Big as a cockroach!"

The old women sucked in their breath. They all started backing off. Frankie got up and walked toward them, still pinching his fingers together. "Look, ladies, did you ever see such a big old bug?"

One old woman screamed. The lady with the umbrella waved it in the air.

George got up then. He started walking toward them. "This one's bigger. See?"

Suddenly the fruit man tore around the counter. "Get out of here, you filthy Gypsy brats!" he yelled. "Get out!"

I jumped to my feet. "Stop it, Frankie," I said. "Come on."

The woman with the umbrella whacked Frankie on the head.

Both boys swung their arms toward the women like they were throwing something. The screaming almost broke my eardrums. George and Frankie were laughing like they were crazy.

The fruit man made a grab for Frankie. But Frankie ducked and grabbed an orange from the stand. He threw it to me. "Catch, Doreen!"

I caught it.

Then Frankie tore down the street with George at his heels. They were still laughing.

I couldn't get past the fruit man. So I had to run the other way. Out of the corner of my eye, I could see a policeman taking off after the boys.

I don't know how long it was before I stopped running. But I was so tired I could hardly breathe.

I scrunched down behind a stack of boxes in an alley to catch my breath. I pulled the stolen fruit from my pocket.

Boy, the orange sure tasted good.

3

Hush, Little Baby

I think I must have dozed off for a few minutes. A buzzing noise startled me. It was some yellow jackets flitting around the orange peels.

I had no idea where I was. But I thought I must have been a long way from home. Some of the buildings had small yards around them. And there weren't any yards in our neighborhood. I could even see a couple of houses down the street.

I hoped the policeman hadn't caught George and Frankie. Then we'd be in a real mess. We'd all have to go to school.

I hated school more than anything. Maybe it wouldn't be so bad if they had separate schools for Gypsies. With Gypsy teachers and everything. But I hated those Gajos.

I hated the way the Gajos acted because they could do things better than I could. I hated getting up in front of the class knowing I couldn't read half the words in the book. Or do any of the times tables on the board. And I hated the way the teacher would shake her head and say, "All right, Doreen. Never mind."

Then the kids would all laugh and whisper. "Dumb ox," they would say when I walked back to my seat.

One time I couldn't hold it back. No matter how hard I tried. I jumped right on top of a girl before I knew what I was doing.

Her name was Hollis Grey. I guess I must have hated her with all my body and blood. It made me hurt everywhere. I hated her orange hair and her freckled face. And her fat knees. And her dresses that were so short her underpants showed. I even hated her name. It wasn't a name at all.

I didn't know any of the take-aways. And the teacher said, "All right, Doreen. Never mind."

When I walked by the girl's desk, she whispered, "Ignorant Gypsy."

I leaped right on top of Hollis. I pulled her ugly hair. I scratched her ugly face. And I kicked her ugly knees.

The teacher called the principal. He pulled me off by my hair and threw me on the floor.

For the rest of the day, I was forced to sit on a chair in front of the class. It was awful. All the kids stared at me.

That was the school where some of us kids got free milk and graham crackers every morning and afternoon. But it was still a bad place.

I begged Uncle Alex not to make me go back after that happened. I told him I wished I wasn't a Gypsy.

Uncle Alex just said, "Keep your head up high, little one. You're as good as anybody. Don't be ashamed of being a Gypsy."

I wasn't. But the Gajos sure were ashamed of me.

It was now afternoon. I was getting hungry, but I didn't want to go home. I wanted to see as much as I could. It might rain again tomorrow. Then I'd have to stay in that dark, musty building all day.

I started walking. I tried to stay off the busy streets. I didn't want the police to see me wandering around on a school day.

After a few blocks, there weren't any big buildings. There were real houses with flowers and trees in the yards. The trees were starting to turn red and gold. They looked pretty. Some of the houses were shabby-looking. But some of them were nice. I saw one that reminded me of the house we stayed in that time.

Two kids were playing in a yard surrounded by a fence. They were pulling a puppy in a big red wagon. It was a cute little puppy. I slowed down to look at it.

The little boy said, "Hello." He was about Nicky's age.

I didn't answer him.

"What's your name?" he asked.

I didn't want to talk to the boy. I just wanted to look at the puppy.

The little girl came up to the fence. "How come your dress is so long?" she asked me.

"Gypsies like long dresses," I said before I realized it.

"What's a Gypsy?" asked the boy.

"Nothing," I mumbled.

"That's pretty," the little girl said.

She was pointing at my ruby necklace. It had been my mother's. And Grandmother said I could wear it if I promised not to lose it.

Just then the door flew open. A woman came out. "Bobby! Jeanie!" she called. "Come here right now!"

An older woman came out too. "Why—I believe that's a Gypsy. Bobby, bring your toys in the house," she said.

I kept on walking. I passed a lot of houses and a few stores. I came to a library. I sat on the steps and rested for a few minutes.

People looked at me funny when they walked by or climbed the steps of the building. I just sat there. I tried not to see them.

I wished Frankie and George were still with me. Frankie didn't mind the Gajos as much as I did. Oh, don't get me wrong. He hated them. But he also thought they were funny.

Frankie was more like Uncle Alex. Uncle Alex said outwitting the Gajos made life worth living. He was good at it too.

I figured I'd rested long enough. So I crossed the street. I began walking toward the park I could see in the next block. I decided that I'd look it over, and then I'd start home. If I could remember the way.

Grandmother and Uncle Alex wouldn't be too worried. Lots of times when Frankie strayed too far from home, he'd sleep in a garage or shed someplace. And he'd just come home in the morning. They knew we'd get back all right.

I'd never seen a nicer park. There were more trees and shrubs than I could count. There was a statue of a man on a horse. And a fountain with water running into a deep pool. I drank some.

I was getting too warm. But I didn't want to take off the jacket. I might lose it. And then Rosa would be mad.

Some people, mostly women, were playing tennis. I

moved closer and watched them for a while. It looked like a lot of fun.

While I was watching, I thought I heard a baby crying. I glanced around. But I couldn't see anything.

Then the crying got louder. I could tell it was coming from the other side of the building by the restrooms. I went over and looked.

Sure enough, there was a baby in a buggy. There wasn't anyone else around. I decided one of the women on the tennis court must be its mother.

I went to the restroom. When I came out, the baby was crying even louder. The women on the court didn't act like they heard it.

I looked inside the buggy. It was a cute baby with curly yellow hair. When it saw me, its eyes got real big. And it stopped crying.

"You've sure got a dumb mother," I told it.

The baby made a cute noise and waved its arms around.

I walked a few steps away. The baby started crying again.

I went back. "Hey," I said. "Don't cry. You're all right."

I jiggled the buggy a little bit. Then I started singing real low. "Hush, little baby, don't say a word. Mama's going to buy you a mockingbird."

It stopped crying, just like that! It started making noises like it was trying to sing too.

"If that mockingbird don't sing, Mama's going to buy you a diamond ring." I sang until the baby fell asleep.

But I didn't get any farther than the fountain. Then the baby started in all over again. I ran back.

"Now stop it," I scolded. "You're nothing but a bawl baby."

The baby stuck its lip out. It looked so sad. So I bent down and kissed it right on the mouth.

I thought I should go find the baby's mother. But maybe she'd get mad. Maybe she didn't care if it cried.

I pushed the buggy back and forth a little. Then the sun got in the baby's eyes. So I moved it down the path a little. It was smiling now. And it was cuter than ever.

"All right," I said. "I'll take you for a little walk. But only a little one."

I didn't mean to walk so far. But before I knew it, I was clear across the park. I'd been singing, and the time went real fast. The baby was sound asleep with its fist in its mouth.

I was just getting ready to take it back when I heard voices coming my way.

It was too late. There were three women with a policeman.

"My baby!" one of the women shrieked. "She's got my baby!"

The policeman stared for a minute. Then he shouted, "That kid's a Gypsy! Hey, you!"

I wanted to tell them I wasn't stealing the baby. That I was only trying to make it stop crying. But I knew better.

I broke into a run. I had never run so fast in my whole life. My heart was up in my throat. It was beating so hard I could hear it.

I'd heard all those crazy stories that Gajos told about Gypsies stealing babies. I knew I couldn't make them believe me in a million years. All I knew was that if they caught me, they'd put me in jail for the rest of my life. Or maybe even worse.

I didn't even take time to look back to see if the policeman was getting close. I just ran until it felt like my legs were going to drop off. And my heart felt like it was going right through the top of my head.

4

Cement Pipes, Ice, and a Dog Named Peppy

It seemed like ten years before I finally stopped running. But I didn't stop because I wanted to. I fell down. And I just couldn't get back up again.

At first I couldn't see anything except colored spots in front of my eyes. The kind you see when you hit your head really hard. All I could hear was my heart thumping. It was so loud that I thought it would break my eardrums!

My whole body was wet from sweating. My leg was throbbing, so I pulled up my skirt to see what was the matter. I had a terrible gash just below my knee. It was bleeding really bad. Plus, it was full of gravel and dirt.

I wiped it off with my sleeve. I tried to pick the gravel out. But it hurt too bad.

I looked around and realized I was close to a train yard. I remembered running across some tracks and falling down a lot.

I was sure I must have been a hundred miles from the park. I listened hard to see if I could hear any sirens. I heard a train whistle. But no sirens.

I also saw big cement pipes all over the place. They were stacked on top of one another. They looked like cave apartments.

I started crying. I didn't want to. I just couldn't help it. I didn't know where I was, I hurt all over, and I was scared to death.

A boxcar bumped into another one. It made a big crash and shook the ground. It scared me so bad! I jumped up and crawled into one of the pipes.

I couldn't stop crying. I cried harder and harder. My nose was running. But I couldn't stop long enough to wipe it. What was I going to do? What was going to happen to me?

Finally I guess I cried myself to sleep. But I didn't really rest. I had horrible dreams. I dreamed I was in a damp, dark cave. And I was holding the baby in my arms.

The baby wouldn't stop crying. I tried to sing. But I couldn't make a sound. There were lice crawling all over in the baby's hair. Everytime I tried to pick one off, it bit me. I didn't have a bottle to feed the baby. So I put a pickle in its mouth. It was screaming its head off.

Pretty soon there were policemen everywhere. They had guns. And they were swearing and calling me bad names. One of them kept saying, "Give me the baby, little girl. I won't hurt you."

He reached for it. He must have touched my sore leg because I jumped and tried to sit up.

"I won't hurt you, little girl. Wake up."

It wasn't a dream voice. It was real. I scooted back farther in the pipe. But something had a hold of my leg and pulled me back.

"Now, now, little girl. I won't hurt you."

I didn't see the man until after I smelled him. It was the worst smell I had ever smelled. It smelled like garbage, sweat, and Grandmother's wine all mixed together.

Then I saw his face. It was all whiskery. His eyes were bulgy and wet-looking. Like the frogs Frankie and I used to catch on the riverbank. He was smiling. But his teeth were real yellow and crooked. There were brown slobbers on his chin.

I tried to get away. But he was still holding my leg. I tried to yell, but I couldn't. I think I was too scared.

"I won't hurt you, little girl," he whispered. It sounded like bubbles in his throat. "You be a good girl, and I'll buy you some candy."

His breath blew right in my face. I felt like I was going to throw up. He put his other hand on the back of my neck. He started to pull me toward him. Then I did throw up. It went all over him.

He jerked back. And I jumped to my feet and started running. I screamed so hard it felt like my throat was tearing.

I didn't even feel the pain in my leg. All I could feel were his warm, damp hands touching me. I could still smell him.

It seemed like I would never see another human being again. There was nothing but boxcars, lumber piles, and rows of trucks and street sweepers.

I knew I'd run straight to the first person I saw. Even if it was a policeman. Nobody could be worse than that dirty old man.

Finally I could see houses ahead. I looked over my shoulder. The man was nowhere in sight. So I slowed down a little.

Then my leg really started hurting. It was bleeding too. I could feel the blood running inside my shoe.

I reached the first block of houses, so I ducked down

an alley. I didn't see anyone. But I could hear a few sounds. A door slamming, a dog barking, and a woman calling her kids home.

At the end of the next block, I saw an ice wagon. It was parked at the corner. I squeezed in between a woodshed and a grape arbor and hid.

I saw the ice man carrying a block of ice into a house. As soon as he was out of sight, I sneaked over to the wagon. I found a chunk of ice just right to carry in my hands.

I squeezed back into my hiding place. Then I sat down on the ground and started sucking the ice. My mouth was as dry as an old bird nest.

Then I put the ice on my sore leg. It felt good. It wasn't bleeding as much now. But it was swollen and puffy.

I reached up and picked a bunch of grapes. It was the first food I'd had since the pickle and orange that morning. That seemed like such a long time ago.

I wondered if I'd ever get back home. If I'd ever see my family again. I could feel a sob coming. But I swallowed hard and reached for some more grapes.

I was so hungry. And I gobbled them so fast my stomach started aching. I twisted around so I could lean against the shed and be more comfortable. The ice melted after a while. Then my leg started throbbing again.

Men were coming home from work and going into the houses. The sun was going down. I knew it would be getting dark before long.

I tried to think of something I could do to make the time pass. If I could sing, it would help. But I didn't dare. Not even softly.

I tried to say my times tables. But I didn't know very many.

I spelled my name over and over in my head. D-O-R-E-E-N. D-O-R-E-E-N. I tried Frankie's name. F-R-A-N-K-. I got stuck. I didn't know if it was *Y*, or what.

My leg kept hurting. I felt my necklace inside my blouse, and I reached for it. It was lucky I hadn't lost it. Grandmother would be furious.

I always thought of my mother when I touched the necklace. I wondered if anything so awful had ever happened to her when she was little.

If she were here now, she would make my leg better. Maybe she'd even hold me in her arms and sing to me. Grandmother said she had a beautiful voice. And she used to sing all the time.

Lights started going on in the houses. It got darker and darker.

Finally I crawled out from behind the arbor. I was so stiff and sore, I could hardly stand up. I took a few steps and almost fell down.

I had to walk. I just had to. It was the only way I

could get back home. And it might take all night to find my way.

But after I'd gone a couple of blocks, I knew I couldn't make it. My leg was too sore. And I was cold.

I'd have to find a place where I could sleep. Someplace that was warm and dry. The sky was getting cloudy. It felt like it was going to rain again.

I stopped behind a pretty white house. A back door opened. A little dog came down the steps.

From just inside the door, a voice cried, "Now, Peppy, you be a good dog. And don't run off, or a big dog will catch you and eat you up."

I ducked into the shadows. I couldn't help smiling. Whoever heard of a big dog eating a little dog? And besides, the woman had a funny voice.

Peppy bounced across the lawn. He sniffed a few bushes. He found one that was just right. Then he discovered me standing there and almost wagged his tail off. "Shh," I whispered. "Go away."

But he didn't want to go away. He snorted and wiggled all over. I squatted down and patted him on the head.

"Hi, Peppy," I said softly. "Are you a good dog?" It was nice to talk to someone. Even if it was a dog. At least I didn't have to be afraid of him. I played with him until the door opened again.

"Peppy," the woman called. "Where are you? Don't you hide from me, you little scalawag."

A nice smell came through the open door. It was something with cinnamon in it. My mouth watered.

Finally Peppy ran to the woman. Then the door closed behind them.

I started to step out of the shadows when the door opened again. This time two women came out. I couldn't see their faces very well. But one of them was short and fat. And the other was taller and real skinny.

The fat one had a flashlight. The skinny one was carrying a box. I could see the tops of fruit jars sticking out.

"Now, Emily," said the fat one, "let me get the cellar door open. Don't drop them and fall, dear."

"I'm not about to drop them. And I'm not about to fall," the skinny one said.

The fat one puffed as she lifted the door to the cellar. They disappeared down the stairway. I could still hear them.

"Don't they look pretty? That's 41 quarts of tomatoes. And 56 quarts of peaches. It looks like 38 quarts of green beans. And let's see, 20—"

"Polly! Don't stand there all night and count. It's cold down here. Hurry up."

The two women closed the cellar door. They went back into the house. I didn't have to wonder where I was going to sleep that night. And I didn't have to wonder what I was going to eat.

It was chilly in the cellar. But not as cold as it was outside. I could hear the rain hitting the two small windows that were above my head.

By the time I finished a whole jar of tomatoes and half a jar of peaches, I was full. Nothing had ever tasted so good.

After a while my eyes got used to the dark. In a corner, I found a pile of gunnysacks and some newspapers.

I spread out the papers and some of the sacks. I used Rosa's jacket and the rest of the sacks to cover up. I snuggled down deep in my bed. It wasn't real warm. But it was better than being out in the rain.

Every once in a while, I could hear the two women upstairs. "Polly, did you put the milk bottles out?"

"Yes, dear, I did," Polly answered. "And I wrote a note for the milkman to leave some butter."

Just before I fell asleep, I heard a piano playing upstairs. Someone was singing, "Shall we gather at the river? The beautiful, the beautiful river—"

The piano music was pretty. But that was the worst singing I had ever heard in my life!

5

The Fruit Cellar

Several times in the night, the pain woke me up. I tried to keep my head under the covers. That way, if I cried out in my sleep, the women upstairs wouldn't hear me.

I'd planned to get up before daybreak and start home. But when I finally did wake up, the morning light was coming through the tiny windows.

I could hear kids on the sidewalk. They were laughing and yelling on their way to school.

"Oh, Emily, dear," Polly was calling from above me. "I'll go down and get some jars while you wash the cucumbers. Maybe we can get all the pickles out of the way today."

My heart jumped in my throat. She was coming down to the cellar! I had to hide—fast. I threw back my covers and jumped up.

The pain in my leg was fierce. I tried to put my weight on it. It hurt so bad that my eyes watered.

"If we finish all our canning today," Polly was going on, "we can start washing the bedding tomorrow. I do so love fresh, clean blankets and sheets on the beds. Pray that the sun shines, dear. Then we can get them all dry before dark."

"If you're going to stand there chattering forever, the sun will be done shining. And it'll be snowing," Emily answered. "We'll be putting up pickles come Christmas."

"Oh, Emily," Polly giggled in her funny voice. "That's not likely. You do fret so, dear. We've got all day. And if we don't finish today, we've got—"

"Polly!"

"All right, Emily. I'm going, I'm going."

The footsteps were right overhead. It must be a kitchen, I thought.

I threw the jacket across my shoulders. Then I piled up the gunnysacks in a hurry. I'd already hidden the jars I'd opened the night before.

My eyes searched the cellar for a good hiding place. In the corner, there was a big old dresser with boxes piled on top. I limped over. And I scooted in behind it.

Part of me stuck out. But it was a dark corner and away from the fruit closet. Please don't let the woman find me, I prayed silently.

Polly opened the cellar door. She was singing and puffing all at once while she waddled down the stairs. "Bringing in the sheaves . . . uh . . . uh . . . bringing in—"

Oh, what a horrible voice! I didn't know what the tune was. But I was sure it wasn't the one she was singing.

I could see her face real plain now. Her hair was as white as white could be. Her eyes looked blue. She had the fattest, rosiest cheeks.

She didn't look very scary. But she was a Gajo. I didn't dare let her catch me.

"Oooh! Don't they look pretty." She was rubbing her hands together. "Nothing is prettier than home-canned fruits and vegetables. My, but those tomatoes are red and plump this year. Let's see now — 41 quarts. Or was it 42? No, I believe it was 41."

She pulled a pair of glasses out of her apron pocket and put them on. She started pointing and counting. "One, two, three—"

I drew in my breath.

"Polly!"

Polly jumped like someone had hit her. She grabbed up a box. And she started cramming jars in it.

"I'm coming, Emily!" she yelled at the top of her lungs. Then real low she mumbled, "Never saw anyone fret so. Poor soul, just a nervous wreck."

I thought she'd never get through. My leg was throbbing and throbbing.

At last the old woman waddled back up the steps. She was struggling with the box of jars.

I limped across the cellar and eased back down on the gunnysacks. After a while I finished the jar of peaches. I never knew time could go so slow. I wished I had some more ice to put on my leg.

Grandmother must be wondering about me. Maybe Frankie and George had told her what had happened. Then she probably thought a policeman had caught me and put me in jail. She would be more mad than worried.

Grandmother sure didn't like policemen. She was forever casting curses on them.

Grandmother was good at curses. Not all Gypsies can do it. Grandmother says you have to have a strong link with the spirits. If you ever make the spirits mad, they take away your power.

Grandmother's ancestors came from Serbia. And the Serbian curse is very strong and hard to break.

One time Grandmother put the bad-luck curse on a truant officer. He had threatened to put her in jail. She was in trouble for not sending Frankie and me to school.

The man only laughed at Grandmother. "Ignorant old witch!" he sneered. "*You'll* find out what bad luck is when the law gets through with you."

But a few days later he was back. It was plain to see that the curse was working. There were circles under his eyes. Like he hadn't slept for a long time. His lips were dry. And he kept licking them. He even looked older. This time he was so polite.

"Please, ma'am," the truant officer said. It was almost a whisper. "I beg of you to lift this awful curse," he said.

Grandmother explained that the curse was a very powerful one. Only a great deal of silver and gold would break it.

"I have no gold and silver," the officer said. "But I'll pay anything. Anything."

It cost him a lot of money. But he was so happy when he left. I could tell he didn't mind at all.

I tried to get my leg in a position where it would stop hurting. It was no use. I tried not to look at it. It was a mess.

I think I cried more that day than I have ever cried in my life. It seemed like years since I'd left home with George and Frankie.

I dozed off a few times. But the noises from upstairs kept waking me. Polly sang a lot.

Some of the songs I knew. So I sang along with her. But I had to be careful not to sing too loudly.

I don't know what time it was. But it must have been late in the day when I heard Emily say, "We need a few things from the grocery store. Let's go now while the jars are cooling. We'll have an early supper when we get back."

"Don't let me forget to get some peppermint candy," Polly said. "I just love peppermint. And I haven't had any all week."

"If you'd cut down on sweets, you'd be better off," said Emily. "You're getting heavier all the time."

"Oh, Emily dear, don't scold. I do so love sweets. And it's no worse to be too fat than too thin."

"Pshaw!" Emily snorted.

I heard them close the front door and walk down the sidewalk. It was dead quiet.

I stood up. I moved around in the small space that wasn't piled with boxes and old furniture. I thought if I exercised my leg, it would feel better.

I needed some more ice. The other ice had helped a lot. Surely there was an icebox upstairs. Anyone who lived in such a nice house would have an icebox.

It was all I could do to push the cellar door over my head. Luckily the back door was unlocked. Peppy came tearing in from another room. He was barking real loud.

"Nice dog," I said. "Nice Peppy."

Peppy remembered me. He stopped barking and wagged his tail.

I lifted the lid on the icebox. Inside was a new block of ice and several small chunks around it. One of them would be just right.

I opened the door in the front. There were all kinds of good things. Sausage, cheese, apples, and a bowl of beans. I gave Peppy a sausage and put another one in my pocket.

Before I left, I looked the room over. It was a huge kitchen. It had a big iron stove in the corner. And a round table right in the middle. The pickles were lined up on the counter. Everything was so shiny and clean. I could even see myself in the linoleum.

I returned to my hiding place in the cellar. Then I took the sausage out of my pocket and ate it. Was it ever delicious. I wished I'd taken another.

By the time the ice melted, my leg felt better. Then I fell asleep.

6

Gypsy in a Flannel Nightgown

At first I thought I was dreaming. It was summer, and I was with my family. We were camping in a grove of willows beside a rippling stream. I was asleep under a warm comforter. And the morning sun was shining in my eyes.

I opened my eyes and blinked. It wasn't a stream

45

rippling. It was rain beating against the windows. And it wasn't the sun. It was a flashlight shining in my face!

"Sakes alive! It's a child—a little girl!"

Polly was behind the flashlight. I flung myself backward. But there was nothing there but a solid wall.

I sprang up. A pain shot through my leg. And I crumpled to the floor. Polly dropped the flashlight. Her soft hands pulled me up and held me while I struggled weakly. I was still numb from sleep.

"Let me go," I sobbed. "Please let me go. I'll go away."

"But what are you doing here?" Polly asked. "Where did you come from?"

She stepped back a little. She looked me all over. I heard her gasp. "Why—child, are you a Gypsy? You look like a Gypsy. You are a Gypsy!"

Polly's hands got tighter. She screamed right in my ear, "Emily! Come quick! There's a Gypsy in the cellar!"

I tried to lift my good leg to kick her in the shins. But I couldn't make it. Besides, Emily was there just like that.

"What's all that fuss?" Emily demanded. "I thought you'd fallen down the—"

Emily broke off when she saw me. "Who's that?"

"A Gypsy!" Polly exclaimed, all excited. "She was sleeping here. A real Gypsy, Emily. Right here in the cellar."

Emily picked up the flashlight. She held it in my face. "Oooh!" She shuddered. "Polly, it *is* a Gypsy!" She waved her hands all over. "Let her go! Don't touch her!"

"Emily, don't talk so," Polly scolded. "It's only a little girl. And there's something wrong with her. She can hardly stand up."

I knew it wouldn't do any good to break away. I wouldn't even be able to get up the steps.

"Help me get her upstairs," said Polly.

Emily hesitated for a moment. Then she got me under one arm while Polly got the other one. They practically carried me into the house. They sat me in a big stuffed chair in the living room.

My eyes darted around the room. A phone sat on a stand. They'd call the police. The police would take me to jail. I'd never get home again!

Polly tried to raise my skirt. "Now, dear, let's see what's wrong." I slapped her hand away.

"Did you ever?!" Emily exclaimed. "She's horrid!"

"She's just scared," Polly said. "You can see she's scared."

Peppy wriggled at my feet. He was trying to get close to me.

"Peppy likes her," Polly said. "He wouldn't like her if she was horrid, would you, Peppy?"

Peppy bounced up and down, yapping.

"See?" Polly tried to raise my skirt again. I let her. When they saw the cut, they really carried on. Even Emily.

"I'll get some salve and something for a bandage," Polly said, starting for the kitchen.

Emily stopped her. "No, I'll get it. You stay here and keep her calm. Don't let her get excited. It could turn into blood poison."

Polly kept patting my hand and making clucking noises. "Poor child. Poor little scared girl. How did you hurt yourself?"

"I—I fell down," I mumbled.

Emily came back carrying a pan of water. And a basket filled with jars, bottles, and bandages. She was practically running. "Pull her skirt up higher. Put her foot on the stool. Take her shoe off. Go fix her a cup of tea." She gave orders left and right.

Polly dashed around. She was huffing and puffing like crazy.

After they bandaged my leg, I drank the tea. Then they began asking questions. One right after the other.

"Where did you come from?"

"What's your name?"

"Where are your folks?"

"What are you doing out so late at night?"

I waited until they got through. I didn't want to tell them about the baby and the police. I didn't think they'd believe me. Especially Emily.

So I just said, "My name is Doreen. We just moved to this city. I went for a walk. I hurt my leg and couldn't find my way home. I was cold. So I snuck down in your cellar."

Emily just stood there, looking at me. But Polly kept saying, "Poor dear. Poor little girl."

"Please don't call the police," I begged. "Let me sleep in the cellar tonight. Then I'll go away in the morning and never come back."

I thought Polly was going to faint. "Sleep in the cellar, indeed! You'll spend the night right here." She patted my head. "We wouldn't think of calling the police. In the morning we'll find your home. Your family must be out of their minds with worry."

I slept in a bed. A real bed with crisp white sheets and a lace bedspread.

As soon as my head hit the pillow, I was asleep. I forgot about all the bad things that had happened. I was warm and comfortable. My leg hardly hurt anymore. Tomorrow I would be back home with my family.

I awoke to the sound of water running. Surely it couldn't be raining that hard. I raised up on one elbow and looked around. It was a nice room with pink curtains on the windows. And bright-colored braided rugs scattered on the floor.

A big dresser with a mirror stood at the foot of the bed. I turned around so I could look in the mirror. That was me! That skinny little black-haired girl in the huge bed. It was hard to believe. I had spent the night in a house with Gajos!

The door opened. Polly came in. She was waddling and smiling all over. "Good morning, dear," she greeted me, half singing it. "Did you sleep well?"

Before I could answer, she went on. "I've got your water run. Let's have a nice bath. You can get all prettied up for your folks."

She took off the bandage before I climbed into the tub. My leg looked much better.

Emily washed my clothes in the sink. And I wore Polly's long flannel nightgown while they dried. The wet clothes were on a clothes rack in front of the heating stove. I was almost lost in Polly's gown.

Polly chuckled. And her blue eyes twinkled. "Where are you, little Gypsy girl? Where are you hiding?"

I couldn't help laughing right out loud. Even if I did feel foolish. Polly looked so funny. The way she wobbled all over when she laughed.

"Don't call her 'little Gypsy girl,' " Emily said. "Call her by her name." Then she turned to me and said, "You can call me Miss Emily and my sister, Miss Polly."

Miss Emily wasn't as friendly as Miss Polly. But I wasn't quite so afraid of her anymore. Even if she did remind me of a schoolteacher.

I had the biggest breakfast I'd ever seen. Oatmeal,

toast with jelly, scrambled eggs, bacon, canned pears, and milk. I could hardly eat it all.

But Miss Polly kept saying, "More, child, more. You're no bigger than a bar of soap after a hard day's wash."

I put my clean clothes back on. Then Miss Emily brushed my hair until my scalp felt like it was on fire. It really hurt. I gritted my teeth but never made a sound.

"I called our neighbor, Mr. French," Miss Polly told me. "He is going to drive us around in his car. That's better than taking a streetcar all over town looking for your home."

Mr. French was a sour-looking old man. I don't think he wanted to take us. He didn't say anything when he saw me. But he looked real funny at Miss Polly and Miss Emily. Then he shook his head.

He sat up straight and stiff behind the steering wheel and puffed his cigar. Every once in a while he sort of snorted. I didn't like him.

He was like all Gajos—stuck-up. Even if he did take us to lunch in a real restaurant. My food would have tasted a lot better if the old man hadn't watched every bite I took.

It was no use looking for my place. All the streets and buildings looked alike. We drove by some neighborhoods where Gypsies lived. But I didn't know any of them.

I sat in the backseat all the way back to the sisters' house. I had to bite my lip to keep from crying. Miss Polly kept hugging me and saying, "Now don't you fret, Doreen. We'll find your people one way or another."

But they didn't. For days they tried everything. They even called the police to see if a little Gypsy girl had been reported missing. I didn't want to tell them that Grandmother wouldn't call the police for anything. They'd just hunt for me on their own.

A few days later I was sitting on the back steps. I could hear them talking in the kitchen. Miss Emily was saying, "We can't keep her here, Polly. She belongs with her own people. We'll have to call the welfare."

"We'll do no such thing!" Miss Polly said. She sounded mad. "They'd put her in an orphanage. They'd starve her and beat her and—"

"Nonsense!" Miss Emily said. "They'd take good care of her. And they'd probably find her folks."

"She stays right here! We'll find them!" Miss Polly said.

Miss Emily argued. But Miss Polly wouldn't listen.

"All right," Miss Emily finally agreed. "But she has to go to school."

Then I'd run away, I thought. I wouldn't go to school. Not for anything. No one was going to make fun of me ever again.

But where would I go? If they couldn't find my home, how could I?

Before I knew it, I just broke out crying. I tore into the bedroom where I slept. The old women came running in all puzzled and worried. So I told them how much I hated school. I begged and pleaded with them not to make me go.

Miss Emily was upset. "Children have to go to school, Doreen." But she talked nicer than I'd ever heard her. "Do you want to grow up to be ignorant?"

"I'm already ignorant," I sobbed. "I can't read. And I can't add and subtract. I can just barely write my name."

"That's because you don't try hard enough," Miss Emily said.

"And because you don't go often enough," said Miss Polly. "You can't learn if you don't go every day."

"School is dumb!" I screamed. I pounded my fists on my knees. "I hate it! No matter what I do, the Gajo kids can do it better. I hate them!"

"Doreen!" Miss Polly gasped. "It's not nice to hate. The Lord wants us to love everyone."

"Then why do the Gajos hate me?" I sniffled and wiped my nose on my sleeve.

Miss Polly handed me her hankie. "My sister and I are Gajos, as you say. And we certainly don't hate you."

I pointed at Miss Emily. "She does," I said.

Miss Emily looked real uncomfortable. "I—I don't hate you, Doreen. I—I guess I just had to get to know you."

I didn't say any more because I could see it made her feel bad. And I thought maybe she did like me now.

I began to feel ashamed of myself. They had taken me into their home. They had been so good to me. My leg was healing up. And I had more to eat than I'd ever had before.

Now they were asking me to do something for them. And how did I respond? Like a big baby.

Right then I made a decision. No matter how much I hated it, I would go to school.

7

Two Foster Mothers

School was just the way I knew it would be. The kids wanted nothing to do with me. They laughed when I made mistakes. And I made a lot of them.

I was put in the fourth grade. So I was older than the rest of the kids. Even if I wasn't any bigger.

The teacher was the same as all the others. When I didn't know an answer to a question, she would shake her head and say, "All right, Doreen. Sit down."

One Friday she told me I should take my reader home over the weekend and practice reading. I didn't want to take the dumb book home. I hid it under my sweater. And I snuck it into my bedroom when I got home.

I thought I had put it in a safe place. But not safe enough. Miss Polly found it when she cleaned my room Saturday morning.

"Oh, Doreen," Miss Polly cried. "You brought your reader home. Come read for us, dear."

"Yes, Doreen," Miss Emily said. "We've been wondering how you're doing."

I made up all kinds of excuses. I told them my eyes hurt. I told them it was a new book, and we hadn't started it yet. But they wouldn't listen.

They settled down on the sofa. Then they put on their glasses. I squeezed in between them. My hands were so damp, I could hardly open the book. I felt sick to my stomach.

I couldn't stand it if they laughed at me. Or worse yet, if they shook their heads in disgust and said, "All right, Doreen. That's good enough."

I knew six words on the first three pages. They took turns saying the other words for me. I scooted lower and lower on the sofa. Finally Miss Emily said, "Doreen, you seem to be having a lot of trouble."

"I think she does very well for such a little girl," said Miss Polly.

"Nonsense," said Miss Emily. "She can't read at all. And it's time she learned."

She pulled me up straight on the sofa. "Now, dear, we're going to start at the beginning. And you'll learn every word in this book."

I couldn't believe my ears! Miss Emily wasn't laughing at me. She wasn't disgusted with me. And she called me *dear.*

All weekend they helped me. They made me read every page over and over again. I didn't remember every single word. But when my turn came to read Monday morning, the teacher smiled at me and said, "That's much better, Doreen."

I was so full of love for Miss Emily and Miss Polly that it was stuck in my throat, and I couldn't swallow. I wanted to do something to show them how much I cared.

All the way home from school, I looked in the store windows. I wished I had enough money to buy some of the nice things I saw. Like the cute cookie jar shaped like a little log cabin. Or the bright yellow tablecloth with matching napkins. If only I had some money. But I didn't.

I could at least pick them some flowers, I thought. I'd seen some pretty ones growing in a vacant lot a few days ago. If they were still in bloom.

I turned a corner and started toward the lot. When I

came to a big red brick house in the middle of the block, I stopped.

The house had a long porch. It went clear across the front and one side. And along the top of the porch wall were dozens of potted plants. All kinds of beautiful plants in colored pots and planters.

Right away I saw the one I wanted for Miss Polly and Miss Emily. It was the biggest. And the pot was covered with foil. It even had a white ribbon around it. Like the ones I'd seen in the flower shop windows downtown.

I glanced around the block. No one was in sight. So I dashed up the steps and grabbed the plant.

It was heavy. But I held it tight in both hands and ran. I cut through the vacant lot and down the alley to our backyard.

Peppy was waiting for me the way he always was when it wasn't raining. He yapped and frisked around my feet. "Don't tell, Peppy," I said happily, "but I have a present for Miss Polly and Miss Emily."

The old women were in the kitchen making bread. I crept in real quiet and yelled, "Surprise!"

I put the heavy pot down on the table. Right next to the breadboard where Miss Polly was kneading dough.

The sisters' eyes got really big when they saw the plant. Miss Polly put her arms around me. She hugged me and got flour all over my clothes. "How sweet of you, dear," she said. "Isn't it nice, sister?"

But Miss Emily was looking at me real funny. "Doreen, where did you get that plant?"

I swallowed hard. "The teacher gave it to me," I said. "She—she gave it to me because I read so well."

Miss Polly hugged me some more. "Now that was nice of her. Wasn't that nice of her, Emily?"

Miss Emily was still looking at me. "Doreen, I want the truth."

"I—I told you," I stammered.

Miss Emily walked over to me. She raised my chin up so hard I had to look right in her face. "We can ask the teacher, you know."

My chin started shaking. Miss Emily raised it up higher. "The truth, Doreen."

My nose started running. "I—I wanted to get you something nice," I whimpered. "I didn't have any money."

I knew I was going to cry. So I ran to my room. I threw myself on the bed.

Miss Polly and Miss Emily waited a little while before they came in. Sniffling and sobbing, I told them where I got the plant.

Miss Polly panted. She put her hands on her chest like she couldn't breathe. "Oh, dear!" she cried. "Oh—oh, you stole it!"

Then Miss Polly turned to Miss Emily. She said real quiet, "She's just a child, sister. Maybe she thought it was all right. You know, they say Gypsies teach their children to—"

"Ridiculous!" Miss Emily cut in. "It doesn't make any difference how old you are. Or who you are. It's wrong to steal."

She sat down beside me on the bed. "Doreen," she said. "Stealing is a terrible thing. The Lord tells us right in the Bible, 'Thou shalt not steal.' "

"But that's not for us," I blurted out. "The Lord was the one who said it was all right for Gypsies."

"What nonsense, Doreen!" Miss Emily gasped. "Whoever heard of such a thing?"

I told her about the Gypsy legend. When Christ was crucified, the Roman soldiers told a Gypsy smith to make four nails for the cross. The Gypsy refused. And the soldiers went to a Jewish smith. When the nails were finished, the Gypsy smith tried to steal them. But he only got one.

The Lord was so grateful for the Gypsy smith trying to help that he gave permission for Gypsies to steal. At least once every seven years. But I didn't tell them that part.

"See, sister?" said Miss Polly. "She didn't know it was wrong."

Miss Emily put her arm across my shoulders. "That's a nice story, Doreen. But that's all it is. A story. I'm sure the Lord did not mean for a nice little girl like you to steal."

I took the plant back. And I promised never to steal or lie again.

I brought home a bouquet of flowers from the vacant lot. They were half-dead. But Miss Polly and Miss Emily said they were the prettiest flowers they had ever seen.

I still didn't like school too much. But it was better than ever before. Miss Emily and Miss Polly helped me every night. And I got pretty good at reading.

Sometimes I would go to the library and check out books. I even began to learn my times tables. I could say the *threes* and *fours* all the way through without making any mistakes.

The kids didn't laugh at me as much as they used to. In the classroom, they treated me all right. But on the playground, they didn't pay much attention to me.

There was one girl who always smiled at me and said hi. But she played with the Gajo kids. I didn't care much. I just waited until school was out. Then I could get home to Miss Polly and Miss Emily.

I'd do my homework as soon as I got home. Then I'd listen to *Little Orphan Annie* on the radio while dinner was cooking. I sure liked Little Orphan Annie. She was a lot like me. But you could tell from the funny papers, she wasn't a Gypsy.

Lots of times after dinner Miss Polly would play the piano. And I would sing. She reminded me of Grandmother, the way she carried on about my singing.

Miss Emily would lean back in her rocking chair. She'd smile up at the ceiling with her eyes closed. I could tell she liked to listen. I was glad because I could sing all day and night.

Once Miss Emily said, "You should have voice lessons, Doreen. You have such a beautiful voice. It should be trained."

I was really happy with the two women. But I did miss my family. Especially at night. Right after I went to bed.

I think I missed Frankie the most. It was a good thing it was me instead of him who ended up with the old women. It would just about kill him if he had to go to school. I wondered if we'd ever see each other again. Maybe he wouldn't even like me anymore when he found out I'd lived with Gajos.

One day when I got home from school, a strange lady was sitting in the kitchen. She was drinking tea with Miss Polly and Miss Emily. Miss Polly's eyes were kind of red. And she jumped up and grabbed me when I came through the door.

"This is Doreen, Miss Winters," Miss Polly said. "We take awful good care of her. You can see we take good care of her, can't you?"

The lady smiled at me a little.

Miss Emily said, "Doreen, Miss Winters wants to ask you some questions. She's from the welfare."

My body stiffened. If Miss Polly hadn't been holding me so tight, I'd have jerked loose and run away. I was scared to death of welfare people. They were even worse than truant officers. They were always threatening to take Gypsy kids away from their folks over the littlest thing.

Miss Winters started asking all kinds of questions about Uncle Alex and Grandmother. I thought some of them were pretty nosy. But I answered all of them I could or wanted to.

Then Miss Emily said, "There are some fresh cookies in the kitchen, Doreen. Get some and go outside and play for a while."

I didn't play. And I gave the cookies to Peppy. "What's going to happen to me?" I asked the little dog. "What if they put me in one of those bad places for kids who don't have a family?"

Peppy didn't seem worried at all. He gobbled down the cookies and begged for more.

After what seemed like hours, Miss Emily called me in. The welfare lady was gone. Miss Polly and Miss Emily were all smiles. They almost squeezed the life out of me.

"You get to stay with us, dear," Miss Polly sang. She danced me all around the room with Miss Emily holding onto one of my arms.

"Yes, Doreen," said Miss Emily. "Until they find your family, this is your foster home. Polly and I are your foster parents."

Miss Polly chuckled. "Just think, Doreen, dear. You have two mothers. A fat one and a skinny one."

"Oh, Polly!" said Miss Emily. But she was laughing too.

8

Spitting Mad

I found out the school had reported me to the welfare. I heard my teacher and some other teachers talking about it in the hall. I was close enough that they could see me. But they acted like I wasn't there.

My teacher was saying that I must feel very out of place in a school with all Gajos. Only she said *white students*. One of the teachers said she hoped they'd locate my family. Or find a suitable place for me. One said they had a lot of Gypsy students in the downtown districts.

"When their families decide to send them, that is," the teacher said. "Their attendance records are very low. But of course, with their limited learning abilities—"

"Yes, but those schools are set up to deal with the situation," another teacher interrupted. "Ungraded classes and special teachers."

"But do they learn anything?" one of the teachers asked.

"Oh, well, it keeps them off the streets," another answered.

Then my teacher said, "Doreen's doing better than I'd expected. And she's really no problem."

"Really!" the other teachers said.

"Really," my teacher said. "So far she's been just fine."

That's what made it worse. Her saying such a nice thing about me.

Miss Polly and Miss Emily overslept one morning. Miss Emily hardly had time to comb my hair. I ate cornflakes and a piece of bread with jam.

"I hate sending her to school without a hot breakfast," Miss Polly said.

Then she found out there was no dessert to go with my sandwich. And she was really upset.

"She'll be fine," said Miss Emily. "Doreen, stop at the grocery and get a package of cupcakes."

She tied a nickel in my hankie. Then she put it in my coat pocket.

Some other kids were in the store. The girl who always smiled and said hi was there. I'd found out her name was Betty. She was behind a grade. She was with another girl from our class.

Betty was buying a pencil tablet. She was trying to decide between one with a picture of Clark Gable or one with Nelson Eddy and Jeanette MacDonald. I liked Nelson Eddy and Jeanette MacDonald best. Miss Polly and Miss Emily took me to see their movie *Rose Marie*. They sang beautifully. It made goose bumps break out all over me.

"I wish they had one of Shirley Temple," said Betty. "I like her."

"I've got Dick Powell," the other girl said. "He's good."

The girl opened her loose-leaf notebook. I moved closer to see. I'd never heard of him.

Betty looked up and saw me. She smiled and said hi.

The other girl moved back. "Well, what are you trying to do, Gypsy girl, steal it?" She looked at Betty like she'd said something funny.

I got so mad that everything went fuzzy. I got hot all over. It felt like little pins were sticking in me. I pushed my foot hard against the floor so I wouldn't kick her.

My fists started to tighten up. And I jammed them in my pockets.

Then just like that, I spit on her. I didn't even know it was coming until I saw it running down her face. I could hear her screaming bloody murder as I ran out of the store.

She almost broke her neck to get to the teacher's desk first thing and tell on me. The teacher made such a fuss, I thought she was going to have a heart attack. She shuddered all over and told me how surprised she was that I'd do such a nasty thing.

After school I had to stay in and write "I WILL NEVER SPIT ON ANYONE AGAIN" 50 times on the blackboard.

I could hear that girl snicker behind my back as she walked out of the room. But Betty touched me on the arm and said, "Good-bye, Doreen."

My teacher didn't send a note home. So Miss Polly and Miss Emily didn't find out. I couldn't tell them. I tried to. But the words got stuck in my throat. I couldn't stand for them to be ashamed of me.

I told them I was late because I had gotten a pain in my side. So I had to walk home real slow. I said I even had to sit on the curb a couple of times when it got bad. It was another lie. But I told myself it was nicer than telling the truth this time.

Miss Polly fixed some hot ginger tea. Then she rubbed me all over with camphor.

"That's silly," said Miss Emily. "How is that going to cure a pain in the side?"

"You never know until you try," said Miss Polly.

My teacher wasn't as friendly for the next few days. Sometimes I'd feel her eyes on me. And when I'd look up, she'd start straightening papers on her desk. Or fix the combs in her hair.

But one recess Betty asked me to jump rope with her. We didn't say anything to each other. But it sure was fun.

The next recess she jumped rope with the girl I spit on. So I played with a dog that was walking around the school yard. He had sores all over him. And the other kids didn't want anything to do with him.

Then one day, the greatest thing happened. I got a 90 on a spelling paper. It surprised me more than it did anyone else. I only missed one word. *Neighbor.* I got the *e* and the *i* backwards. I got the *gh* right, though.

The teacher wasn't mad at me anymore. "I'm very proud of you, Doreen," she said, smiling.

None of the other kids got a grade that high. Most of them failed it. And the teacher was disappointed in them. "There's no excuse for it," she said. "Look how well Doreen did. The rest of you should have done better."

Miss Polly and Miss Emily were so proud of me. They put the spelling paper up on the kitchen wall. Then they took me to the ice cream parlor. They bought me a strawberry milk shake. It was so big that I could barely get my fingers around the glass.

It was raining when we left the ice cream parlor. It seemed like it rained all the time. I never did like the rain very much. I could hardly wait for winter to be over.

As soon as spring came, our family always loaded our things into Uncle Alex's pickup and moved back to the country.

But what if I never found my family again? What if I spent the rest of my life with Miss Polly and Miss Emily?

I was happy there. And I loved both of them. But I'd miss roaming around the country with my family. Camping out, sleeping under the stars.

I didn't understand how Gajos could be happy living in one place all the time. Houses were nice and comfortable in the winter. But how terrible it must be to live inside in the summer. To never go anywhere or see anyplace but your own neighborhood. Especially if it was in the city.

I'd have to find my family before spring. Even though I knew I'd miss Miss Polly and Miss Emily something awful. I felt like I had two families. And I wanted to live with both of them.

The more it rained, the more homesick I was. Miss Polly noticed something was wrong with me. She decided I needed a good tonic. She bought some bad-tasting stuff from the Watkins man. She made me take it with cream of tartar.

"You'll kill that child with all that junk you pour down her," Miss Emily said. "Land sake! Her poor stomach will explode."

"Now, sister," replied Miss Polly. "It's for her own good. You can tell something's ailing her. And there's nothing like a good dose of cream of tartar to purify the blood."

I didn't know about it purifying my blood. But it sure puckered my mouth. I thought when she and Grandmother meet someday, they should exchange remedies.

It stopped raining for a few days, and I felt better. Miss Polly swore it was her doctoring that did it, though. She even claimed my voice sounded better than ever. And she had me singing all the time.

"You'll be another Marian Anderson one of these days," she said.

"Who's Marian Anderson?" I asked.

Miss Polly acted surprised. "Only one of the most famous singers in the world," she answered.

I smiled just thinking about it. It must be wonderful to be a famous singer. I wondered if Marian Anderson was a Gypsy.

9

Popcorn Balls, Cake, and a Giant Toothache

One Saturday morning Betty came over. Was I ever surprised to see her. I'd already eaten breakfast. And I was getting out of the tub.

Miss Polly came bouncing into the bathroom. She was talking so fast, I could hardly understand her. "Someone's here to see you, dear. Hurry and get dressed fast."

"To see me? Who?" I couldn't imagine who would be here for me.

"Somebody," Miss Polly said in a teasing way. "I won't tell."

She was almost rubbing off my skin with a towel.

"I know!" I shouted. "The welfare lady! She found my family!"

"No, no, dear, it's somebody else. Somebody who wants to play with you."

Play with me! Then it had to be a kid. Maybe somebody new in the neighborhood. Probably some little kid who didn't go to school yet.

Miss Polly pushed me down on the toilet seat. She started brushing my hair like mad. She almost pulled it out by the roots. She tied the sash on my dress and said, "Go see who it is."

I felt funny. I didn't want to just rush out. If it was somebody I didn't even know, I wouldn't know how to act.

Miss Polly kept shoving me. She was more anxious than I was.

Betty was sitting on the edge of the sofa. When she saw me, she smiled and said hi.

Then I said hi. I didn't know what else to say, though.

Miss Polly shoved me again. She said, "Now you two go out and play. If it starts raining, come inside.

I'll go bake a cake, a chocolate one with chocolate frosting. I'll fix some popcorn balls too."

You'd think having a girl come to play was the grandest thing in the world. I guess it just about was.

Miss Polly hurried off to the kitchen. She was humming to herself.

Betty said, "I can stay as long as I want. I brought my yo-yo."

"I'll get mine," I said. I got my jacks too.

We sat on the front porch for a while and played jacks. We didn't say a whole lot. But we giggled when one of us missed. I won three games, and she won three games.

Then we played with our yo-yos. Betty was really good. She could walk the dog, hang the old man, and spin out. I could barely walk the dog. I always got knots in the string.

Then we got tired of playing. Betty asked, "Do you want to go for a walk?"

We walked for about an hour. She pointed out where different kids lived. She knew most of the ones in the class.

"That's where Bernard Kowalsky lives," Betty said.

I knew who he was. But I couldn't say his name. He was the biggest boy in the class.

"There's Jesse Burley's house," Betty pointed.

"Who's he?" I asked.

"You know, the boy who stutters," she said.

I remembered. He stuttered in the classroom. But not out on the playground.

"And that yellow house is Joyce Moore's," Betty pointed out. "Her dad owns a shoe store. Shall we see if she wants to play?"

I said no. I didn't know her very well. Besides she was the smartest kid in the class. And smart kids were always extra stuck-up.

We passed Jack Tulley's house. He bit his fingernails and never tied his shoes. He gave me a piece of cake out of his lunch one day. But I thought that it was a trick. So I threw it in the wastebasket. I wasn't going to be fooled by any Gajo.

"That's where *she* lives." Betty was pointing at the white house on the corner. It had red shutters and a picket fence around it. It was the house I'd always liked.

"Who?" I asked.

"Carol Ross—the girl you spit on," she said.

My face got hot. I wished Betty hadn't said that.

Betty and I started back home. I didn't like the white house on the corner anymore.

Miss Polly had hot cocoa to go with the cake and popcorn balls. She'd made vanilla pudding too. Three desserts all at once! She had her best tablecloth and glass plates on the table.

"Golly!" Betty exclaimed. "It looks like a party."

"That's what it is, dear," Miss Polly said. "You come next Saturday too, and we'll have another party. And bring along some other children."

I didn't want Betty to bring anyone else. But I didn't say so. She was the only really nice one in the class. All the others made me feel uncomfortable.

Miss Emily was glaring at Miss Polly. But Miss Polly wasn't paying any attention. She was having too much fun. "Doesn't everything look good," she said.

"Good enough to rot every tooth in their mouths," Miss Emily grumbled. She made Betty and me eat a peanut butter sandwich first. "Put something decent in your stomachs anyway," she said.

Betty acted like she was a bit scared of Miss Emily.

Most of the time I liked peanut butter. But right then it tasted like mud. I was sure glad Miss Polly liked sweets so much.

Betty said she'd had a good time. And she would come back a lot.

I could hardly wait for Monday morning to come. I hoped Betty would tell the kids about coming to my house. Maybe she'd play with me every recess from now on.

But when Monday came, I didn't go to school.

I guess Miss Emily was right about all those sweets. Because my tooth started aching on Sunday. And it wouldn't stop.

Miss Emily and Miss Polly tried everything. They put cloves on it. They poked aspirin down me. I stayed on the sofa all day with a hot water bottle on my jaw.

Sunday night the sisters took turns getting up with me. My tooth hurt all night.

I felt terrible Monday morning. Miss Polly was going to try something she had read in a magazine. It was supposed to be good for a toothache. But Miss Emily said they weren't going to fool around any longer. "She has to see a dentist," she said. "It's got to be filled or pulled."

The minute Miss Emily said that, I was sure it didn't hurt as bad as it had before. I'd never been to a dentist in my life. But I'd heard some kids talk about it. It sounded worse than having a toothache. I was scared to death.

"I think my tooth is better," I said.

Miss Emily said, "That's a natural reaction, dear. Now, you be a brave little girl."

I tried awful hard to be brave. But I was terrified. All the way downtown on the streetcar, Miss Polly tried to make me feel better. She held my hand. And she squeezed it as hard as she could. "It's going to be all right, dear. He'll freeze it so you won't even feel it."

"Freeze it!" I said. "How can you freeze a tooth?"

"They stick a needle in—" Miss Polly began.

"Polly!" Miss Emily jabbed her in the ribs with an elbow.

Finally we got to the dentist's office. I was so scared that they had to lift me into the chair. When the dentist looked in my mouth, he made a face. He said my teeth were in bad shape. They needed a lot of work.

He stuck a thing that looked like Miss Emily's crochet hook in my tooth. The pain went clear to my toes. I wanted so bad to bite his hand. Then he stuck me with the needle—four times. I thought the needle must have come out the back of my head.

After a while my whole face fell asleep. My tongue felt as big as a pillow. Then I saw the dentist pick up the big pinchers off the table. I squeezed my eyes as tight as I could. And I held my breath.

"Look there, Doreen," Miss Polly said. "There's the bad old tooth that was making you hurt so."

I opened one eye. The tooth was hanging in the pinchers. It was all bloody and had a hole in it. I threw up.

The next day I felt good. But Miss Polly said I should stay home one more day. "If you go out in the cold air, you'll catch a cold in your tooth," she said. "Then you'd be a mighty sick little girl."

I drank soup, tea, and fruit juice all day. Every hour I rinsed my mouth with warm salt water. I was sure glad to get rid of that dumb tooth.

That afternoon Miss Polly taught me a new song. The name of it was "The Bells of Saint Mary." It was real pretty, and I loved to sing it. She played the piano while I sang. Miss Emily said she'd never heard anything so beautiful in her life.

I guess I was singing so loud that I didn't even hear somebody at the door. The next thing I knew, I looked up, and there was my teacher. She was standing there, listening to me.

My teacher's eyes were as big as saucers. She looked like she was in a trance or something. "Why— why—" she said. "I had no idea this child could sing like that."

"Prettiest voice you ever heard," Miss Polly said. "Sings like a bird, doesn't she?"

"Indeed, she does," my teacher agreed. "I've never known of such talent in a child so young."

They kept on until I got embarrassed. I thought what they were saying about me was nice. But it still made me feel uncomfortable.

My teacher had been wondering why I wasn't in school. That's why she'd come to the house. I think she thought I'd played hooky. She put her arm around me. She said, "Doreen, you must promise me you'll sing that song in our school program. It's a week from Friday."

I went numb all over. "I—I can't," I whispered as loud as my voice would go. I'd die if I had to sing in front of all those people. I just knew I would.

"Nonsense!" said Miss Emily. "You can. And you will. God didn't give you that voice to hide in a paper sack."

"Oh, Miss Emily," I begged, "please don't make me. I can't."

"Of course you can, dear," Miss Polly said. "You can do anything you set your mind to. Sister and I will come to hear you. Won't we, sister?"

"We wouldn't miss it for the world," answered Miss Emily.

Before my teacher left, it was all settled. I was going to sing in the program. And it was just a week and a half away. I knew that all the begging in the world wouldn't change my foster mothers' minds.

"She'll have to have a new dress," Miss Polly said. "Organdy, with a velvet sash."

"Blue," said Miss Emily. "With polka dots."

"I think yellow would be nice," Miss Polly said. "She'd look so sweet in yellow. With her dark hair and eyes."

"All right, yellow," Miss Emily agreed. "But polka dots."

"Sister," said Miss Polly. "Wouldn't it be nice if she had a pair of black patent leather sandals?"

"I don't see how we can afford it, Polly," Miss Emily said.

"Oh, Emily, we can, can't we?" Miss Polly begged. "We could cut down on something. I'll drink black coffee. And we won't have to buy cream. We can use margarine instead of butter and—"

"All right, all right," Miss Emily cut in. "She'll have her shoes."

"Oh, won't she look pretty?" exclaimed Miss Polly. "We'll have to get some film. We'll take a whole roll of pictures. Maybe she'll have her name and picture in the paper."

"Now, sister," Miss Emily chuckled. "Don't get carried away."

It would have been so wonderful any other time. A new dress and new shoes all at once. And a whole roll of pictures of just me. I'd never had my picture taken before.

But I thought I'd rather wear rags and go barefoot for the rest of my life than have to stand on a stage in front of all those people. Singing for Miss Polly and Miss Emily was one thing. But up on a stage in front of all those Gajos!

10

Itchy! Itchy! Itchy!

Betty spent all her recesses playing with me now. Most of the time we'd jump rope. But if it rained, we went in the gym and climbed the ladder bars. I couldn't chin myself as well as Betty could.

Once in a while another kid would play with us. I told Betty I'd really rather play with just her. And she said okay, if that's what I wanted.

I liked Betty more all the time. In my secret mind, I pretended she wasn't a Gajo. I pretended she was a Gypsy. Like me.

Itchy! Itchy! Itchy!

Betty was excited that I was going to sing in the school program. "I can't do anything," she said. "I can't sing, or dance, or play any instrument."

I didn't care. She was my friend. And I liked her just the way she was. Even if she was really a Gajo.

Miss Polly and Miss Emily couldn't keep their minds on anything but that program. They worked on my dress every day. But they spent more time taking it apart than anything. Because they couldn't agree on it. Miss Polly wanted it smocked. And Miss Emily said that was for little girls. She wanted me to look grown-up.

"But she's not grown-up," Miss Polly argued. "She is a little girl."

"She'd rather look grown-up," said Miss Emily.

I didn't care how they made it. I knew it would be beautiful. It was yellow organdy with white polka dots. The velvet ribbon for the sash was white too.

I had never seen such shoes in my life. They were black sandals with satin bows like tap shoes. Miss Polly and Miss Emily made me break them in. I had to wear them around the house every day. I tried to walk without bending my toes. I didn't want any cracks in them. Nothing could be as pretty and shiny as those shoes.

My teacher knew I was worried about the program. She kept telling me not to be scared. She knew I'd do fine.

She started asking me a lot of things about my folks. I didn't know if she was being nosy or not. I think she was just asking because she didn't know very much about Gypsies.

One day she wanted me to talk to the class. She wanted me to tell all about my people and the way we lived. I didn't want to. But I didn't want to hurt her feelings. After all, she'd been pretty nice to me.

I showed the class my necklace. I explained how it had been handed down all the way from my great-great-great-grandmother who had lived in Serbia. The girls all crowded around me. They were begging to try it on. But I had to push them away. I didn't want any Gajo touching my mother's necklace.

The boys liked the thought of traveling around the country. They thought camping out in the summer would be great. I didn't tell them that we usually lived in a store building in the winter. I knew they'd laugh.

One of the girls wanted me to tell her fortune. But the teacher said we didn't have time for that in the classroom. I told them about our music and our dances. When I finished, all the kids clapped. I got embarrassed.

This school was sure a lot nicer than any I'd ever gone to before. I bet even Frankie would have liked it a little bit.

One day Betty was absent. Some girls asked me to play hopscotch with them at recess. I didn't know them very well. And I wasn't very good at hopscotch. But I played anyway. Everything was just fine until along came Carol Ross, the girl I had spit on. She had to stick her big nose in.

She just stood there, watching for a few minutes. Then Milly, one of the girls I was playing with, asked, "Do you want to play, Carol?"

"With a Gypsy?" Carol snorted.

I could feel my face getting hot. I tried not to pay any attention. I tried to ignore her.

"Be quiet, Carol," said Milly. "Do you want to play or not?"

I held my breath. I was waiting for her answer. I wished she'd just shut her mouth and get out of there. But she started scratching herself all over. Then she said, "I wouldn't play with a Gypsy." She scratched harder. "I itch something awful every time I get around her."

One of the girls put her hand over her mouth and giggled. Carol scratched harder than ever. She started chanting, "Itchy! Itchy! Itchy!"

I got the maddest I'd ever been in my whole life. So mad I felt like I was on fire. I flung myself at her. I pounded her face with both fists. She was screaming her head off. But she didn't even try to hit back.

I guess I would have hurt her something awful. Maybe even killed her. But I heard my teacher yelling, "Doreen, stop it! Stop it this instant!"

My teacher and another teacher were running toward us. I would have stopped and let my teacher do whatever she was going to do to me. But the other teacher grabbed my arm. She almost pulled it out by the roots.

"Gypsies!" she roared. "They're all alike! Nothing but dirty, savage animals!"

I gave her a kick in the leg that hurt my foot. Then I took off running as hard as I could go. I ran clear across the playground toward the street.

Everything was blurry. I was so full of hate that I was ready to explode. I hated everything and everybody. I hated all the Gajo kids in that school. I hated the teachers. I even hated Miss Polly and Miss Emily for making me go to that awful place. I hated my family for not finding me. I hated my mother for dying when I needed her so much.

I thought it was the teacher screaming at me. But it must have been the squealing of car tires. I didn't even see that car until it was almost on top of me.

11

Tear-Stained Get Well Cards

It was strange waking up. I felt like I was floating in space. My leg hurt. And it felt like I had two heads. I opened my eyes. But it was so bright that I had to close them again.

I thought someone was saying, "Doreen, wake up, sleepyhead."

I decided I was dreaming. I opened my eyes again, slower this time. I'd never seen so much white.

The walls and ceiling were white. The curtains and bedcovers were white. It was like being inside a giant snowball.

I moved my head real slow so it wouldn't break. There was a face right close to mine. When I realized it looked like Uncle Alex's face, I knew I was dreaming. I blinked my eyes as fast as I could. But the face didn't go away.

"Hey, lazybones," the man said.

It was Uncle Alex! Just like that, I was in his arms. We were hugging each other. And I was laughing and crying all at once. It was a long time before either one of us could say anything.

Then Uncle Alex held me back and looked at me. "I was so frightened when I heard what had happened," he said. "When I first saw you here in the hospital, you were so still and pale. I thought you were dead."

Uncle Alex squeezed me. "You were very lucky," he said. "Only a bad bump on the head and a bruised leg, the doctor said. But it took you so long to wake up. We were getting worried."

I thought it must have been because I was so miserable. I didn't want to ever wake up again.

"I thought I would never see you again," I said.

Uncle Alex's eyes got teary. "We thought you were gone forever, little one," he said. "Your grandmother has been sick with missing you and worrying so. Then yesterday a friend told me he had heard about the accident. I went to the police. And they told me where to find you."

Uncle Alex stopped long enough to give me another hug and kiss. "The two kind old ladies told me everything that has happened," he said.

I had almost forgotten Miss Polly and Miss Emily. "Where are they?" I asked.

"I insisted they go home and rest," Uncle Alex answered. "They sat up all through the night with you."

I told him how wonderful Miss Polly and Miss Emily were to me. "I'll miss them so much. You will take me to see them sometime, won't you?"

"Of course, little one," Uncle Alex assured. "We are very grateful to them for their kindness."

When Uncle Alex said, "I'm so happy you have been going to school," it brought everything back.

"I'm never going back!" I cried. "I'm not going to any school again! Not ever!"

I told him how awful it was. How the kids had acted. The bad things the teachers had said. "I hate them all— except Betty. And they all hate me."

Uncle Alex looked puzzled. "That's very hard to believe," he said. He was motioning to the far wall.

I turned my head toward the long table under the window. I gasped and sat up straight in bed. I had never seen so many flowers. It looked like a florist shop.

"But—but—" I stammered. "Where did they come from?"

"From everyone," Uncle Alex answered. "From some of your classmates. From some of the teachers at the school. From the grocery where the old ladies trade. From their neighbors. The yellow daisies in the blue vase are from Betty. There's even a plant from the man who was driving the car that hit you."

I guess I would have broken down right then. But Uncle Alex picked up a stack of envelopes from the nightstand. He dumped them on my lap. "This doesn't look like everyone hates you," he said.

I couldn't believe it. They were letters and cards from kids at school.

The kids had made the cards themselves. They had colored them with crayons. One had a funny picture of a clown riding in a race car. Inside it said, "Get well FAST! Love, Jack Tulley." He was the boy who had given me a piece of cake out of his lunch. I felt ashamed when I remembered how I had thrown it in the wastebasket.

One card had red roses all over it. It said, "Pretty flowers for a pretty girl. Your friend, Joyce Moore."

She was the smartest kid in the whole class. I always thought she must be stuck-up. Being so smart and pretty too.

There was one from Milly, the girl who had tried to make Carol Ross behave herself. And of course, a special big one from Betty.

When I finished reading all of them, I started bawling. "I thought everybody hated me," I cried.

Uncle Alex took me in his arms. Then he rocked me back and forth like I was a little baby. "That's because you expected them to," he said softly. "And because you had made up your mind to hate them."

"But a lot of them said bad things—" I sobbed. "They called me names and—"

"I know, I know," Uncle Alex said, smoothing my hair. "It's because we are a little different, Doreen. Some people don't understand. When you're different, it makes it a little harder.

"But remember. There will always be people like Carol Ross and some of the teachers in the schools. But there will also always be people like your teacher, your friend Betty, and Miss Polly and Miss Emily."

I felt so good inside I could hardly stand it. I kissed Uncle Alex ten times. Then I fell asleep.

When I awoke, it was lunchtime. Miss Polly and Miss Emily were there. There was more hugging and kissing. Uncle Alex kept thanking them over and over. And telling them how much he appreciated what they had done.

I gulped down my soup, pudding, and milk. I wished I had more. It seemed like a week since I'd had anything to eat.

When the nurse came after my tray, the doctor was

with her. He pinched my cheek the way doctors do to kids. "How's my girl today?" he asked.

I told him I was fine. And I wanted to go home.

"Well, we'll see about that," the doctor said. He shined a flashlight in my eyes. He made me put my finger on my nose and look cross-eyed at it. Then he scratched his fingernail across the bottom of my foot.

"I don't see any reason why you can't go home tomorrow," the doctor said, smiling. He pinched my cheek again. "If you promise not to run in front of any more cars."

I promised, and he left. "I'm going home!" I squealed. "I'm going to see Grandmother and Frankie and Aunt Wanda. But . . . but, I'll miss you so much. I won't ever forget you as long as I live."

I was talking so fast I couldn't stop. I was afraid I'd start crying if I did.

Miss Polly's eyes were getting redder and redder. Miss Emily was sniffling. I could feel my nose running. Then we all started crying. Even Uncle Alex. Miss Polly hugged me. Miss Emily patted my head. It was the saddest time of my whole life.

Suddenly Miss Emily said, "But she can't go now. Not until after Friday night. You'll let her stay until then, won't you?"

Uncle Alex looked puzzled.

Then I remembered the school program. I watched Uncle Alex's face while they told him about it.

"We made her a new dress. And we got her new shoes just for the occasion," Miss Polly said. "Please say you'll let her."

Uncle Alex looked like he had something stuck in his throat. "You—you mean Doreen is going to sing in a program? And people will come to hear her?" he asked.

Uncle Alex looked at me like he'd never seen me before. He pulled me close to him. "I'm so proud of you, little one," he whispered in my ear. Then he broke out laughing. "She can only sing if her family can come to see her."

That was that. But no one had asked me what I thought about it at all.

Uncle Alex had to work the next day. So it wasn't until late afternoon that he came after me. He took me to Miss Polly and Miss Emily's house. On the way he told me about the good job he had fixing cars that had been in wrecks.

By spring when it would be time to leave the city, Uncle Alex would have enough money to buy a better pickup truck. It sounded nice. I could hardly wait for spring.

The old women made Uncle Alex stay for supper. They fixed a real special meal. I was so proud of Uncle Alex. He was so handsome. Miss Polly and Miss Emily thought so too. I could tell by the way they looked at him.

After Uncle Alex left, I was so tired. I went to bed early. I had a hard time going to sleep, though. This would be the last night. The last night I would sleep in this pretty room. Tomorrow I would be back home in the dark, musty store building. But I would be with my family.

Just before I fell asleep, I heard Miss Polly crying in the next room. "Now, now, sister," Miss Emily was saying. "Be thankful for the happiness she brought into our lives. Even if it was for just a little while."

I wiped my eyes on the corner of the pillowcase.

The next day was happy and sad. Here I had finally discovered that I had made friends. And now I was going to leave them.

Joyce Moore made me promise to write to her. Jack Tulley gave me some cookies from his lunch. I ate them this time. Milly and some other girls asked me if I would tell their fortunes before I left. I did at recess. I let them try on my necklace too.

I said good-bye to Betty all alone. She just said, "Gee," when I told her I would have Uncle Alex bring me to visit her someday. She gave me her new yo-yo. And her favorite book, *Little Orphan Annie and the Jewel Thieves.*

My teacher was sorry I was leaving. But she said it was nice that my uncle had found me. She told me she hoped I would keep going to school every day because I was doing so well. I said I probably would.

Miss Emily fixed dinner early that night. But nobody ate very much. I was so nervous I couldn't hold still while Miss Polly got me ready. She had to tie my sash three times because I was squirming so. She said it was worse than trying to dress Peppy. I was really going to miss Peppy too.

Miss Polly and Miss Emily found an old suitcase in the cellar. They said I could have it. I couldn't believe I'd collected so much in such a short time. It seemed like we were all talking more than we usually did. I guess it was so we wouldn't start crying again.

12

Singing to the Whole World

When we got to the school, the windows were lit up.
There were a lot of cars parked out front. I'd never seen
the school at night before. It looked different.

Miss Polly and Miss Emily kissed me. Then they
went out to find seats.

My teacher took me behind the stage. The other kids
were waiting there. She said, "You look lovely,
Doreen. That's a beautiful dress."

Some of the kids smiled at me. How could they be
so calm? I wondered. I sat down on a stool.

A teacher came in and said, "Children, I want you to do your very best tonight. Remember, we want our parents and friends to be proud of us."

My mouth felt like it was full of sand. My knees kept bumping together. I could hear my heart beating and my teeth chattering. Someone started playing the piano in the auditorium.

"Ready?" the teacher said. "You're first, Bernard." She helped him put his accordion straps on his shoulders. "There you go," she smiled.

He marched right out on the stage. He didn't act like he was one bit scared. He played "Under the Double Eagle." And he only made three mistakes.

Next Joyce Moore played "Dewdrops" on the violin. She didn't make any mistakes. She never did.

A big boy from the eighth grade whistled like all kinds of birds. He was pretty good. I never could learn to whistle.

Then a girl tap-danced. And someone yodeled and played the guitar. I didn't like the yodeling very much.

It seemed like I'd been sitting on the stool for hours. I felt like a statue. Finally my teacher came in and put her hand on my arm. "You're next, Doreen," she said.

My teacher helped me get to my feet. I tried to walk. But my legs turned to rubber. I couldn't go out there in front of all those people. I just couldn't. Something awful would happen. I'd make a fool of myself, and they'd all laugh. I started to turn back.

"I can't," I whispered. "Please—I can't."

"Of course you can, Doreen," the teacher said. "Now don't be afraid, dear."

Joyce reached out and touched my arm. "You'll do fine," she said. "I know you will."

"You can't do any worse than I did," Bernard chuckled.

My teacher took my hand. She led me to the center of the stage. When she left, I almost followed her. There must have been a million people sitting out there in those seats. I tried not to look at them. My whole body was trembling. My heart was banging against my eardrums.

The piano started playing. I took a deep breath at the place where I was supposed to start. I opened my mouth. But nothing came out.

The piano started again. I raised my eyes a little. I could see Betty and Jack sitting with their families. They were smiling. Right in the front were Miss Polly and Miss Emily.

Right behind them was Grandmother. She glanced around to see if anyone was looking. Then she waved. She was wearing her best gold earrings and a new shawl I had never seen before.

It was so good to see her again. Uncle Alex was there with Aunt Wanda, Rosa, and the boys. Frankie was sitting on the edge of his seat. His hair was all slicked down. He even had on a tie. It must have been Uncle Alex's because it hung almost to his knees.

Suddenly he raised his hand and made a circle with his finger and his thumb. He was grinning like everything at me.

I smiled back at him. Then I took a deep, deep breath. I started singing. For a moment there was nobody in the building except Miss Polly, Miss Emily, and my family.

All at once my knees stopped shaking. My voice grew stronger. I could hear it echoing back from all over the auditorium. From the four walls. From the ceiling. I couldn't believe it. It had never sounded so good!

Miss Polly and Miss Emily were dabbing their eyes with their hankies.

I sang louder. I knew I had never sung like this in my whole life. I lifted my head higher. I looked out across the room at all the people. Everyone was looking right at me. No one was moving or making a sound. A nice, warm feeling went all through me.

This is me, I thought, Doreen. I'm singing to a whole room full of Gajos—and they're all listening. I'm singing to the whole world.

Gypsy in the Cellar
By: Taylor, Bonnie Highsmith
Quiz Number: 2208
ATOS BL: 2.9   F   IL: MG

Word	GL
cellar	3
chuckled	3
kids	3
necklace	3
pickle	5
probably	3
promised	3
sash	5
sausage	4
scolded	4